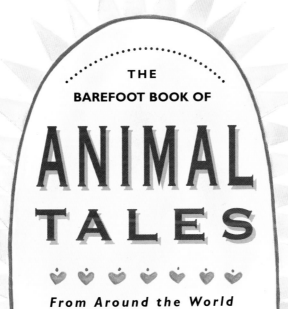

THE
**BAREFOOT BOOK OF**

# ANIMAL TALES

*From Around the World*

Barefoot Books
294 Banbury Road
Oxford OX2 7ED

First published in Great Britain in 1996 by Barefoot Books Ltd.
This paperback edition printed in 2006

The text for 'Grandmother Spider' has been adapted from Alida Gersie
and Nancy King's *Storymaking in Education and Therapy*, published by
Jessica Kingsley Publishers, London.

The art for this book was rendered in watercolour and crayon
The book was typeset in Monotype Imprint 12pt on 22pt leading

Graphic design by designsection, Frome
Printed and bound in China by Printplus Ltd
This book is printed on 100% acid-free paper

Paperback ISBN 1-84686-012-1

British Cataloguing-in-Publication Data:
a catalogue record for this book is available from the British Library

7 9 8

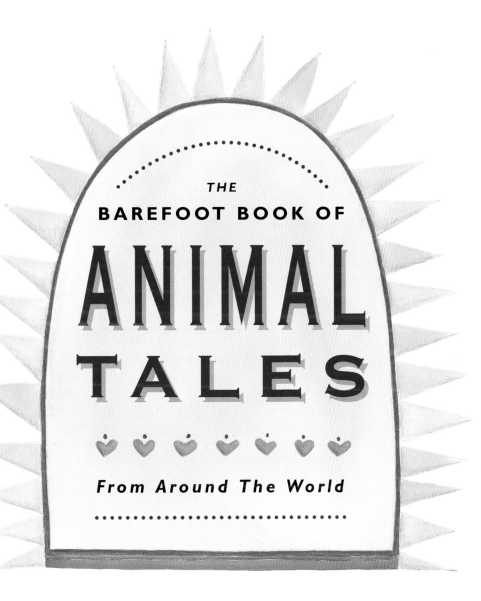

# THE
# BAREFOOT BOOK OF
# ANIMAL
# TALES

*From Around The World*

Retold by **NAOMI ADLER**

Illustrated by **AMANDA HALL**

Barefoot Books
*Celebrating Art and Story*

*for my beloved friend Margaret Button – N. A.*
*for Jean and John – A. H.*

# CONTENTS

# GRANDMOTHER SPIDER

USA

Long, long ago there were only animals living on the earth. The lands of the north were covered in darkness. For millions of years the animals were content to live in this darkness. However, there came a time when they realised that they were always bumping into one another; they were always falling down holes in the ground; they were always stumbling as they ran about. There came a time when they could bear it no longer, so they decided that something must be done about living in such darkness.

Wise Owl declared, 'Let us have a gathering of all the animals in the Northern Lands.'

A special place and time were appointed for the meeting. Animals arrived from far and wide, all bringing their ideas and their hopes.

Wise Owl called out, 'What shall we do, my brothers and sisters? It is always dark here and times are becoming difficult. We must make changes, but how?'

Old Crow was the first to speak out, 'I have heard on my many flights that there are animals on the other side of the world who live in the light.'

Great Bear asked, 'What is the meaning of "light"?'

Old Crow replied, 'Where there is light animals can see all around them. They can see the whole countryside. They can even see each other.'

The animals of the dark place became very excited by Old

Crow's words. They all said, 'We must have this light, so that we too can see where we are going.'

Old Crow continued, 'Maybe the animals of the light place will share some of this light with us?'

Brother Fox called out, 'No, no! I am sure they will not want to share the light with us. This light must be very precious. We shall have to steal it and bring it back here.'

Brother Otter popped his head out of the water and said, 'It's all very well, but who will go to the place of light? The journey is long and dangerous.'

The bravest and strongest animals began to argue. They all insisted that they were the fastest, or the most cunning, or the most clever. At last Brother Possum spoke up above all the noise and quarrelling. 'I shall go, my brothers, because I can hide the light under my bushy tail and so bring it to our dark space.'

Finally, all the animals agreed that Brother Possum should be the one to go. Brother Possum set out on his long journey to the land of light on the other side of the world. The journey was full of dangers and difficulties, but Brother Possum was very determined and very curious. On and on he journeyed. As he came closer to the place of light, his eyes began to hurt – he had not expected such brightness! He screwed his eyes up tightly to protect them. Even today, if you look closely at a possum, you will see his eyes are almost closed.

At last, Brother Possum arrived at the centre of the light. He carefully took a piece of light and placed it under his bushy tail. Then he started his journey home. But the light under his tail was so hot, so fierce, that it burnt all the bushy fur off his tail, leaving nothing but skin and bone. Even today, if you look closely at a possum's tail, you will find it is nothing but skin and bone.

By the time Brother Possum arrived back at the Northern Lands, the light had all vanished. The animals were waiting for Brother Possum. The animals were waiting for the light. How very disappointed they were when they saw him return empty-handed.

Brother Buzzard spoke out, 'I shall go to the land of light and I shall bring some light back.' Brother Buzzard flew high into the sky so that no one would see him when he arrived at the other side of the world. The flight was long and tiring. Finally he reached the centre of the light space. Brother Buzzard hovered around the light and dived down with such speed he was able to take a little bit of light and place it on top of his head. Then he started his long flight home.

The light balancing on top of his head was so hot, so fierce, that it burnt a bald patch. Even today, if you look closely at a buzzard, you will see a bald patch on his head.

By the time Brother Buzzard arrived back in the dark land, the light had vanished. The animals were waiting for Brother Buzzard. The animals were waiting for the light. How very disappointed they were when they saw him return empty-handed.

The animals were very sad. They cried out, 'Our strongest and bravest brothers have tried and have failed to bring us some light. We are still in darkness!'

Suddenly, they heard a tiny, creaky voice, 'Excuse me, brothers. You have tried your best. Now it is time for your sister to go and get the light.'

The animals looked all around them, trying to discover who the speaker was. But they could not see anyone. 'Who is speaking?' they called out.

'It is I, Grandmother Spider,' the voice answered. 'I am very old and very small, but I have a good plan. I would like to try to bring back the light from the other side of the world.'

The animals were sure that Grandmother Spider could not possibly succeed, but they agreed to give her a chance and let her go.

Grandmother Spider scuttled to a place deep in the earth that was rich with clay. She took a little piece of clay and moulded it into a small pot, with a lid which fitted perfectly. She then took the pot, holding it with one of her eight legs, and she started her long journey to the other side of the world, to the place of light. All the while she was spinning her web, leaving behind her a trail, so that she would find her way home.

Grandmother Spider arrived at the centre of the light. She took a small piece of light and put it into her pot. She secured the lid tightly, so that the light would not escape. She started her long journey home, following the web trail she had left behind. Even today, if you look carefully at a spider's web, you will see that it is just like the rays of the sun.

The animals were waiting for Grandmother Spider. The animals were waiting for the light. As soon as she arrived back in the land of darkness, Grandmother Spider asked the animals to form a circle all around her. Then she lifted the lid of her pot, and there was light all over the place of darkness. It was of such radiance, such splendour, that the animals were amazed. From then on, there was day and there was night in the Northern Lands.

The animals were overjoyed. They could now at last see where they were going. They had a great celebration, with singing and dancing, in honour of Grandmother Spider. As for Grandmother Spider, she retreated quietly into the forest from whence she had come. She climbed a tall tree and began to spin a web. Even today, if you look very carefully, you will see that she is still spinning.

# THE RABBIT IN THE MOON

INDIA

Have you ever looked up at the moon, when she is full and bright? Have you ever wondered what that silver-blue shape is on the moon surface? This shape, if you look carefully, has the long ears and the body of a rabbit. Even the little bob tail is there.

Next time there is a full moon, do take the chance to look deeply and silently and then you may very well see the most delightful of animals, the rabbit, looking back at you.

You may ask, how did the rabbit get up there? And, why is it a rabbit when there are so many other animals to choose from?

Once I met an old Indian storyteller and she told me how it was that the rabbit ended up on the moon.

A very long time ago, in a distant land called India, there was the most beautiful forest that you could ever imagine. There were trees of every shape, size and shade of green. There were flowers on the forest floor of such magnificence, releasing such sweet, sweet smells. The trees were laden with every kind of fruit and blossom. Birds and beasts had lived in that forest for thousands and thousands of years.

Among all the animals that lived in this enchanted forest there were four who became the best of friends. They were the monkey, the otter, the young elephant and the rabbit. These four animals loved each other dearly. But, most of all, they loved the rabbit. In fact, all the animals of the forest loved the rabbit more than anyone else in the world. You see, the rabbit was a very special being. She was wise and fearless, she was generous and pure. But most of all, she had a heart of gold. Very often you could see the rabbit sitting in the middle of the glade surrounded by all the animals of the forest. She would tell them wondrous stories. She would tell them of the power that plants and flowers have to heal and restore. She would tell them of the power that love and kindness have to transform. She would tell them of the stars and the planets and of the energies and the magic that is all around.

Even the most fierce of all the animals would come to such gatherings. The tiger came and so did the crocodile. The wolf came and so did the vulture. The rabbit didn't just speak of beautiful things and glorious powers but she lived them too. Her kindness and gentleness shone from within her like the light shines from the moon. And all who came close to her were inspired by her presence.

And so it was that her three closest friends began to change. The monkey, who had always been naughty and mischievous, planning tricks and teasing everyone, now became more considerate and helpful to others. The otter, who had always been so greedy and kept all the fish for himself, now began to share and became helpful to others. The elephant, who had always been so secretive, never telling the other animals where the springs and water holes were, now began to share her knowledge and became helpful to others. And as for the rabbit, she also became even kinder and the glow of

kindness from her heart shone even brighter than before.

One day, the rabbit had a brilliant idea. She called her friends. 'I have a suggestion to make. We have so much food and water between us. We have so much love and friendship between us. Why don't we offer our skills and our food to the world around us? There are so many beggars and so many hungry children, let's offer them a little of ourselves.'

At the very instant the rabbit was speaking, the great heavenly spirit was passing by and heard every word she said. He could hardly believe his own ears, so he decided to pay great attention to what would happen next.

The rabbit continued, 'Look, my friends, look at the moon dressed in all her radiance, shining silver rays across the darkness of night. With her light she transforms the darkness into clarity and brightness. We could do the same with the power of our love and kindness. We could transform sadness and hardship. Let us bring happiness to whomever enters the forest tomorrow.'

The others agreed it was a splendid idea. That night, sitting under a tree covered with red blossoms in the light of the full moon, the four animals made plans for the next day.

The otter made a vow to catch fish and give all his fish away. The monkey made a vow to pick ripe mangoes and give all his mangoes away. The elephant made a vow to find a new spring and give the water away. And so they fell fast asleep. But the rabbit she simply couldn't get to sleep at all, but thought and thought what she could give. 'My only food is green grass, which most creatures do not enjoy. I have nothing at all to give a stranger.' All night long she gazed up at the full moon thinking and thinking of what she could give. Just before her eyes finally closed, a terrible thought came to her. She remembered that humans love to eat the flesh of a rabbit. She took a deep breath and made a vow to give herself away. A great feeling of warmth and joy came over her, and the little rabbit too fell asleep.

The heavenly being was listening all the time and he heard this amazing vow. He decided to come down to earth disguised as a beggar and put the rabbit to the test. It was so remarkable that a mere rabbit would offer such a wondrous thing as selflessness.

Next day, while the creatures of the forest were all resting under the shade of the leafy trees, they heard a voice calling out in the distance, 'Help me, please help me, I'm lost in the forest, I'm hungry and I'm thirsty.'

On hearing these cries the animals ran towards the beggar.

'Don't worry, dear man,' they said. 'We shall take care of you, we shall feed you, we shall bring you water and we shall help you find your way.'

The monkey instantly jumped upon a mango tree and brought down an armful of big red juicy mangoes. He placed the mangoes before the beggar.

The otter instantly dived into the river and caught several plump silver fish and placed the fish before the beggar.

The elephant instantly ran to the new spring and drew out a trunkful of clear sweet water and brought it for the beggar to drink and to bathe in.

The rabbit instantly placed herself before the beggar and said, 'Make a strong fire and I will jump into it so that you can eat of my flesh.'

The great spirit in disguise was astonished at this bravery.

He snapped his two fingers and made a strange sound with his voice. And there before them was a roaring fire. The rabbit, without thinking another thought, jumped into the blaze. But not a hair of her soft fur was burnt, not an inch of her body was scorched, for in that very instant the heavenly being caught the rabbit in the palm of his hand, saying, 'Such love and such courage is beyond anything I have ever witnessed on earth. This selfless deed must be told to all the world. I shall place you, my little rabbit, in the moon, for all to see, for all to learn, for all to remember. You shall appear with every full moon and your power of kindness and love shall shine in the silver light of the moon across the whole wide world.'

With these words he lifted the rabbit into the sky and placed her on the moon where she still lives to this very day.

So, dear children, next time the moon is full, go out and look at the night sky and there you will see for yourselves the very rabbit I have told you about. And you may remember the story and you may remember that if you give something precious away you may receive something back that is very special.

21

# THE DRAGON AND THE COCKEREL

CHINA

There was once a time when dragons were not yet fully formed and when cockerels had tails like those of peacocks and antlers like those of stags. It was during those ancient times that this story occurred.

The celestial emperor ruled over the sky, the sea and the earth. Every New Year, he held a great celebration up in his heavenly palace in the sky. Important guests from the many different stars and planets were invited, among them the animals of the earth.

The animals of the earth loved going to this yearly event up in the sky and they spent many weeks busily preparing themselves, making themselves as beautiful as could be.

Only Dragon was miserable. He felt himself to be the most dull

22

and boring creature in all China. You see, in those days Dragon had the head of a camel, the eyes of a demon, the neck and body of a snake, the legs of a tiger and the claws of an eagle. But the fact that he had nothing on top of his head caused him the greatest shame.

One day, as Dragon was swimming in the river, Cockerel came strutting by. Cockerel looked magnificent with his gorgeous tail fanned open and those huge antlers on top of his head. Dragon looked longingly at the antlers.

'If only I could have such a splendid head-dress, then I wouldn't look so dull any more,' he thought to himself.

Suddenly, he had a bright idea. He called out to Cockerel, 'Hello there, Cockerel!'

'Good day, Dragon! Why do you look so sad?' asked Cockerel.

Dragon replied, 'I am so sad because I have nothing to wear on my head when I go to the New Year celebration. Will you lend me your antlers, please, Cockerel?'

24

Cockerel was amazed. 'Certainly not. I am also invited to the party and I need to wear my antlers myself.'

Dragon said, 'But Cockerel, you look so beautiful with your gorgeous tail. Your antlers only detract from your splendour.'

'No, no, Dragon! I need my antlers,' shouted Cockerel.

At that moment a very distinguished carp raised her head out of the water. She had heard the entire conversation and since she was rather fond of Dragon she said, 'Dragon is quite right, Cockerel. You are indeed more dazzling without your antlers. They do seem to detract from your splendour. Why don't you lend them to Dragon and I shall guarantee their safe return?'

In the end, vain Cockerel was persuaded that he was even more beautiful without his antlers. Cockerel agreed, 'All right, I shall lend you my antlers for one day and one night. You must return them as soon as the New Year celebrations are over.'

Dragon promised that he would.

That night at the New Year celebrations everyone admired
Dragon. Even the celestial emperor gave him a special welcome,
inviting him to sit beside the throne, a place of great honour.
Dragon had never experienced such attention and such admiration
before. He discovered a new part of himself and he liked it very

26

much. Dragon felt a glow all over his body.

However, Cockerel was extremely jealous when he saw Dragon held in such great esteem and he wished he had kept the antlers for himself. Very early the next morning he rushed over to the river where Dragon lived.

He called out, 'Dragon, give me back my antlers!'

Dragon appeared out of the water looking splendid with the huge antlers on top of his head. He said, 'Dear Cockerel, you look so dazzling without the antlers and I look so dull without them, please let me keep them a little longer.'

'No!' cried Cockerel. 'Give them back at once!'

But Dragon had no intention of keeping his promise. 'I must go now,' he said. 'I have very important matters to attend to at the bottom of the river.' And he dived into the water, leaving a furious, screeching Cockerel on the river bank. 'Dragon, give me back my antlers! Dragon, give me back my antlers!'

Carp raised her head out of the water, wondering what all the fuss was about.

'What's the matter, Cockerel?' she asked.

Cockerel replied, 'Dragon will not give me back my antlers and it's all your fault, Carp. You guaranteed their safe return.'

'I'm sorry, Cockerel. I had no idea that Dragon would become so attached to the antlers. I had no idea that Dragon would look so splendid with the antlers. I had no idea that Dragon would be so transformed by the antlers,' said Carp. And she dived back into the

deep water, leaving a furious, screeching Cockerel on the river bank, calling out 'Cockadoodledoo! Cockadoodledoo!'

So when you next hear a cockerel calling out at dawn, 'Cockadoodledoo! Cockadoodledoo!' you will now know that he is calling out, 'Dragon, give me back my antlers! Dragon, give me back my antlers!'

As for the dragon, he became China's most revered creature. The celestial emperor bestowed on him the gift of flight, and the guardianship of all the waters in the sky, sea and earth.

The dragon also became the keeper of the magic pearl – but that's another story. Even today, the dragon is invited to celebrate the Chinese New Year and dance the Dance of the Dragon with the people of China.

# THE GREEDY FROG

AUSTRALIA

Before Dreamtime the earth was dead. There were no mountains, no rivers, no animals, no people – it was dark and dry, there was no rain, no wind, only silence and emptiness. Then something began to change. Dreamtime came to be, and wonderful and strange things began to happen. The world was being created. The rainbow serpent came down from the sky and as he slithered across the world, the earth began to move. Mountains rose and valleys appeared. The earth cracked and rivers flowed. Slowly the earth was covered with trees and plants, flowers and herbs. Animals were blown in by the great winds.

In those days when the earth was green and beautiful there lived a gigantic frog. His name was Tiddalick. Now this frog was

so huge, he was bigger than the
rocks, he was bigger than the mountains.
His giant body loomed between the sky and the
earth. When he was in a good mood all was peaceful
and all was calm on the earth. But when he was in a bad
mood the earth would tremble, rocks would fall and
mountains would shake. Even storms would rise and raging winds
would howl.

One morning Tiddalick woke up in a very grumpy mood. In
fact, he was so grumpy that when he went down to the lake to
drink, he drank and drank until he had drunk up all the water in
the lake. He then edged his way to the river. He drank and drank
until he had drunk all the water in the river. The greedy frog went

on drinking day and night. He
drank all the water from the billabongs,
and the streams disappeared into his vast
mouth. He drank up all the water in the land. He
drank more and more until there was not a drop of water
left in all the world.

Tiddalick was so full he could hardly move, he was so full he
could hardly hop, he was so full he could only sleep. He closed his
great, yellow eyes and fell fast asleep.

The land was parched, the rivers were dry, the land was
cracked. The rivers turned to dust. The animals were dying. The
trees dried up, the leaves drooped, the flowers faded. There was
no movement on earth, no sound.

With their last bit of strength, the animals gathered together in great distress. They cried, 'Tiddalick has every drop of water in his belly. We have nothing to drink, we have nothing to eat. There is no rain, there is no water. What shall we do?'

The wise old wombat said, 'Let us go one by one and plead with Tiddalick to give us back our water.' One by one, the animals went to Tiddalick. The first one was the kangaroo. She said, 'I am the kangaroo, the joyful, jumping kangaroo. But now I have no strength left to jump, all I can do is lie in the dust. Please give us back our water.'

Then the dingo came. 'I am the dingo who barks and howls in the night. I have no strength left to bark. All I can do is lie in the dust. Please give us back our water.'

Then came the kookaburra. 'I am the kookaburra. I tell funny stories and jokes. I have no strength left to joke. All I can do is lie in the dust. Please give us back our water.'

But it was no good. Tiddalick didn't even open his eyes. It seemed that very soon all the animals would surely die; the greedy, grumpy frog would be the only one left alive.

The animals thought and thought about a way to solve this

problem. They were just about to give up and lie in the dust and die when a small voice said, 'I have an idea.'

They all got up and looked around. There was the little bandicoot flapping his large ears.

He continued, 'If we could only make Tiddalick laugh, then all the water from inside him would blow out of his mouth.'

So the animals mustered up their very last little bit of strength and made a circle all around the giant frog's resting place. Hundreds and hundreds of animals came, also the birds and insects, to see if any of them could make Tiddalick laugh.

First the kookaburra told his funniest stories. Everyone else laughed and laughed, but Tiddalick didn't. He didn't even open his eyes.

Next the emu and the kangaroo jumped over each other again and again, round and round in a circle. Everyone else laughed and laughed, but Tiddalick didn't. He didn't even open his eyes.

Then the lizard came and made the funniest faces, sticking out his tongue and turning round and round on his hind legs. Everyone else laughed and laughed, but Tiddalick didn't. He didn't even open his eyes.

The animals called out, 'Come on, Tiddalick, laugh, you big, fat, bloated, squelchy frog. If you could only see yourself you would laugh till you cried.'

It was hopeless. The animals thought that they were doomed and they gave up all hope of ever drinking again.

Just then they heard a strange, tiny cry, 'Let me try, let me try.' It was Noyang the eel, driven from his favourite creek by the drought. He slithered up to the fat, gloomy frog and began to dance. First his movements were slow and graceful, soon he danced faster and faster, wriggling and twisting, making himself into the weirdest and funniest shapes. Coiling like a spiral, then jumping up and uncoiling in the air, bouncing, twirling, he finished by jumping onto the frog's fat tummy and whirling and whirling, spinning round and round like Wurrawilberoo the whirlwind.

Tiddalick started to quiver. The quiver got larger and larger until it became a giggle, the giggle got larger and larger until it became a gurgle, the gurgle got larger and larger until the whole

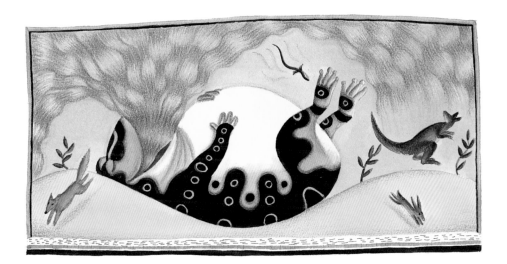

earth shook and trembled. All at once he burst out laughing. The
animals ran for shelter as the water came gushing out of his mouth
like a waterfall tumbling down a mountain.

Tiddalick laughed until every drop of water was out of his belly,
flowing away, filling up lakes and ponds, swamps and rivers.

Once again fresh life appeared all over the earth. The whole
world woke up as if from a deep sleep. Animals and birds, plants
and trees began to move and go about their work as before.
Slowly, the earth became beautiful again.

Ever since that time the Aborigines know when there is going
to be a drought because they see little frogs, descendants of
Tiddalick, filling themselves up with water and then burying
themselves in the ground, waiting for the rains to come again.

# THE MUSICIANS OF BREMEN

GERMANY

A long time ago, there was a farmer who had a donkey that served him faithfully for many long years. While he was able to, the donkey carried sacks of grain to the mill and sacks of flour and potatoes to the market. However, as the years passed, the donkey grew old and weak and could no longer serve the farmer as he used to. The farmer planned to send the donkey far, far away for ever and ever. The old donkey heard of this plan and was very sad that this was to be his reward for years of faithful service. The donkey didn't want to go far, far away for ever and

ever; he knew the farmer planned to send him to the knacker's yard! So, one night, as he was standing in the middle of a green field, he looked up at the moon. She was full and glowing. He closed his eyes and said, deep, deep inside himself, 'I must find a solution, I must find a solution. Please, great moon, shining so brightly, please can you help me to be free?' The very moment that he opened his eyes again, a thought came to him. He knew exactly what he was going to do.

'Of course,' he cried. 'I will run away. I will run along the road to Bremen and become a musician.'

The donkey felt a great wave of warmth inside him. He felt a great strength inside him. He started running across the field and with all his might he jumped over the fence. He was out! He was free! He trotted along the road to Bremen. He was on a journey towards a new life, a new chance. The old donkey was happy. He set off along the road into the wide world singing as he went.

On and on he went along the road, until all of a sudden he saw something by the wayside. It was an old dog. A very sad old dog.

The donkey asked, 'Why are you so sad, Dog?'

The dog replied, 'Every day I grow older and weaker and I can no longer round up the sheep for my master as I used to. So he is planning to send me far, far away for ever and ever and I don't want to go far, far away for ever and ever.'

'Well!' said the donkey. 'Why don't you run away with me to Bremen and become a musician?'

'Yes, please, I'd like that,' said the dog, wagging his tail.

So the old donkey, followed by the old dog, set off along the road into the wide world, singing as they went.

On and on they went along the road until all of a sudden they saw something in the distance. It was a very, very sad old cat sitting on a milestone beside the road.

The donkey asked, 'Why are you so sad, Cat?' The cat replied, 'Every day I grow older and weaker and I can no longer catch the mice in the house. So my mistress is planning to send me far, far away for ever and ever and I don't want to go far, far away for ever and ever.'

'Well!' said the donkey. 'Why don't you run away with us to Bremen and become a musician?'

'Yes, please,' said the old cat, jumping onto the road and

stretching her body.

So the old donkey, followed by the old dog, followed by the old cat, set off along the road into the wide world, singing as they went.

On and on they went along the road until all of a sudden they saw something in the distance. It was a very, very sad old cock perched on top of a farm gate.

The donkey asked, 'Why are you so sad, Cock?' The cock replied, 'Every day I get older and weaker and I no longer wake up my mistress on time in the morning. So she is planning to send me far, far away for ever and ever and I don't want to go far, far away for ever and ever.'

'Well!' said the old donkey. 'Why don't you run away with us to Bremen and become a musician?'

'Yes, please,' said the cock, flapping his wings and jumping down onto the road.

So the old donkey, followed by the old dog, followed by the old cat, followed by the old cock, set off along the road into the wide world, singing as they went.

41

On and on they went along the road until they were so tired they could go no further.

The donkey suggested, 'Let's spend the night under this big oak tree.' The donkey leaned against the trunk, the dog and the cat lay down in the moss at the foot of the tree and the cock flew high up and perched on a branch. Before he went to sleep, he looked around the countryside. He saw a little spark of light in the distance. He called out to his companions,

'There is a cottage over there, friends, and it's not far away.'

The donkey said, 'If that is so, we had better get up and go towards it, for it's not very comfortable in this place.'

And the dog continued, 'Yes, indeed! A couple of bones with meat on them would be very acceptable.'

The donkey, the cat and the cock all agreed that a little hay, fish and corn would not come amiss after such a long journey. So the four friends set out in the direction of the light.

They went on until they reached the cottage. The donkey went right up to the window and looked in.

'What can you see there, Donkey?' asked the inquisitive cock.

'I can see a table spread with food and drink and around the table seven robbers,' replied the donkey.

'That sounds just right for us,' said the dog.

'Yes, yes, I wish we were sitting there,' said the donkey.

The cat asked, 'But how are we going to get rid of those robbers?'

42

The donkey turned his head upwards and looked at the moon; she was full and glowing bright in the dark sky. He closed his eyes and said deep, deep inside himself, 'I must find a solution.' The old donkey then opened his eyes and at that very moment it came to him in a flash; he knew exactly what they must all do.

'I have a plan,' he said.

The donkey placed his forefeet upon the window ledge and called out, 'Dog, sit on my back! Cat, sit on Dog's back! Cock, perch on Cat's back and when I give the signal, we shall all make music.'

This done, they were all ready for action. Donkey gave the signal and the music began.

The old donkey brayed with all his strength, the old dog barked, the old cat miaowed and the old cock crowed. They made such a tremendous noise that the window panes splintered and crashed. The cock went flying into the cottage, after him jumped the cat, after the cat, the dog and, last of all, the old

donkey went tumbling into the room.

The robbers were so frightened by the musicians' unearthly sounds, they jumped up thinking that a huge monster had burst in on them. They dropped everything, took to their heels and were off as fast as they could run into the forest.

The donkey and his friends sat at the table and ate and drank to their hearts' content. As soon as they had finished they put out the light and each animal found a suitable sleeping place. The donkey stretched upon some straw, the dog lay behind the door, the cat curled up on the hearth near the warm ashes and the cock perched up on a beam which ran across the room. Exhausted by their long walk, they were soon fast asleep.

The robbers in the forest were not asleep at all. They were watching and waiting at a distance. When all was quiet and the light went out, they became braver. The chief robber sent one of his men to see what was happening in the cottage.

All was still and quiet as the robber slipped through the open window. He saw a pair of eyes shining by the hearth, and he thought they must be some glowing embers. He needed light, so he held a match to the glow, expecting the match to take fire. Instead, the cat flew in his face, spitting, hissing and scratching him all over. The robber was so afraid that he made for the door. The dog sleeping on the mat by the door woke up and bit the robber as hard as he could in the calf. As he limped over the straw where the donkey was stretched out, the donkey kicked him so hard with both hind legs that he flew right over to where the cock was perched. The

46

cock screeched madly, 'Cockadoodledoo, cockadoodledoo!'

The robber ran back to the forest as fast as he could, crying out, 'We must get out of here. The cottage has been taken over by a huge monster with finger nails like those of a witch and huge teeth like those of a lion and hooves like those of the devil and a voice as terrible as the wind.'

The robbers were so afraid that they all ran away as fast as they could, never to return to the house again.

As for the four friends, they stayed in the cottage, making the short journey every day along the road to Bremen, where they became very famous musicians.

If you should ever be in Germany, do go to the beautiful town of Bremen where you will see in front of the Town Hall a statue of a donkey and standing on his back a dog, and standing on the dog's back a cat, and perched on the cat's back a cock, in memory of the four old animals who ran away from death and journeyed along the road into the wide, wide world, looking for a new life, a new chance...and found it.

# NEVER TRUST A PELICAN

**M**any, many miles away there is a land of great beauty, where the people dance and sing the animal stories they have heard told, over and over again, by the village storyteller.

Many moons ago, there was in this land a very beautiful lake. It was surrounded by a deep, green forest and high mountains. A mighty river flowed into the lake, a river that came from a spring in the mountains, a river that journeyed far and wide over rocks and cascades, tumbling down waterfalls and winding its way until it reached the beautiful lake. The lake was full of life, full of plants, full of frogs and fish and even crabs.

Now there was also a lone pelican living alongside the lake. This pelican had lost his family and friends long, long ago. Now he was old and feeble and lived by the side of the lake all alone. Every day the pelican waded his way into the deeper water to catch the little, juicy fish that swam by. But now that he was getting older and weaker he was finding it more and more difficult to catch the little, playful fish. Most days the pelican went home hungry and miserable. He realised that he would soon starve to death if he didn't catch a single fish.

One bright day, the pelican was staring into the water wondering how he could make a plan to catch the fish without so much effort. Suddenly, upon seeing his own reflection in the water and recognising what a wonderful and clever bird he was, a tremendous and most cunning idea came into his head.

'Yes!' he laughed out loud. 'That's exactly what I will do!'

So the pelican put his plan into action.

The pelican stood by the side of the lake looking very sad indeed. He wasn't even tempted to try and catch the fish swimming past him. The creatures of the lake noticed how very sad the pelican was and they began to wonder what had happened to him.

The old crab, who was the wisest and most courageous of all the creatures of the lake, came up to the pelican and asked, 'Why are you so sad, Pelican?'

'Oh dear, oh dear, oh dear me,' replied the pelican. 'There are such bad times coming to this lake, such great danger is coming to all of us animals.'

'Dear me! Dear me! What is this great danger? Please tell me,' said the crab.

'Indeed, we are all in very great danger,' proclaimed the pelican. 'Soon no more water will flow down from the mountain.

The river will cease to tumble over the rocks and the lake will dry up to nothing. We will all die and vanish.'

The crab was most alarmed and passed on the news to the fish and frogs. The fish were even more alarmed. After all, the pelican could fly off and the frogs could hop off and the crabs could creep off sideways. But what about the fish? They could neither fly, hop nor creep.

The poor fish panicked and swam round and round in circles wailing, 'What will become of us and our little babies, what will become of us?'

The largest and fattest of all the fish then came up to the pelican and said, 'Dear Pelican, you have indeed given us very bad news. But you are a clever chap, please tell us how we can save ourselves.'

The pelican replied, 'I am only a bird, but I may be able to

help you in a very small way.' He continued, 'There is another lake even larger and more beautiful a little distance from here. This lake has a never-ending spring in the centre of it. The water there will never stop, the lake will never dry up. I can take you there if you wish.'

'You are indeed a good friend,' said the fish. 'You can save us. Please take us in your beak to that other lake.'

'It is an extremely difficult task,' said the pelican. 'But I will do my best.'

When they heard this all the fish began to cry out, 'Take me first, take me first.'

'Be patient,' said the pelican. 'I can only carry a few of you at a time. But I shall make as many journeys as I need to. I am very old and feeble now and I may need to have lots of rests between journeys so this task may take some time. But I do promise to save you all.'

The pelican chose the plumpest of the fish, seized them in his beak and flew off to the other side of the deep, green forest. He landed on a large rock and there in peace and quiet he ate them all up, leaving only a few fins and bones on the rock.

He then returned for more. He only had to say, 'Who is next?'

'Me, me, take me,' called the fish.

So he seized more fish and flew them to the rock where he gobbled them up too.

Whenever the pelican was full, he rested and slept in the lovely, warm sun. Whenever the pelican was hungry, he flew back to the lake where more fish were eagerly awaiting their turn to be rescued.

Now, one day, the oldest and wisest crab began to wonder about this great danger. He was very different from the fish, you see; he had travelled a great deal and had seen many things and had learnt many things too. He began to realise that if the water was still flowing so strongly from the mountain then the story of the drought was surely not true. In that case the pelican could not be trusted.

The oldest and wisest crab decided to find out what was going on. So the very next day when the pelican arrived at the lake and called out, 'Who is next?', the crab said,

'Take me, take me, dear Pelican.'

The pelican was delighted, he was getting rather bored with so many fish. He suddenly developed a taste for crab meat and readily agreed.

'I am at your service; come, I shall take you to the new lake.'

The pelican seized the crab in his beak and flew over the deep, green forest to the large rock on the other side.

The wise, old crab looked down expecting to see a beautiful lake. But no, all he saw was a large rock covered with fins and bones. He knew at once what had happened.

The crab was afraid. He realised instantly that the pelican would land on the rock, kill him and eat him up. Just as he had done with all the fish. The crab thought and thought. What could he do to save himself and all the remaining fish in the lake?

All at once he seized the pelican round his neck with his strong pincers. The pelican struggled, flapped his wings in a panic and tried his utmost to rid himself of the crab. But the crab held tight, pressing harder and harder on the bird's neck. Soon the pelican fell to the ground like a heavy stone and that was the end of the pelican.

Slowly, the crab made his way back to the lake, creeping sideways, as crabs usually do, all the long journey back. When he finally reached the lake, the fish were very surprised to see him.

'Why have you come back? And where is the pelican?' they all cried out. The old crab then told them how the pelican had been cheating them and how he had put an end to the pelican...

From that day to this, frogs, fish and crabs have never made friends with pelicans.

# THE MONKEY'S HEART

KENYA

A long time ago in Africa there lived an old tortoise who had a very strange and wonderful dream about a magical tree that grew all the fruits of the earth. She told her friends about her dream and they all set off in search of the tree's secret hiding place. Tortoise led, Lion followed, then came Hippopotamus, Giraffe, Elephant, Monkey, Zebra, Hyena and Gazelle. They searched high and low until one day they reached the secret place where the tree grew. It was the most beautiful sight the animals had ever seen, a tree with every fruit of the earth. Tortoise said the magic word to bring down the fruit and the animals ate as much as they could. Just as they were about to go home, Tortoise proclaimed,

'Each one of us
must take a different seed and plant
it in the earth so that fruit trees of every kind
will grow all over the world.'

And this was exactly what all the animals did.

Monkey took a mango seed and planted it in his favourite spot
by the river. When the mango tree was fully grown, it produced
the most delicious mangoes. Monkey made his home in that
wonderful tree and enjoyed its juicy fruit.

Being a friendly and generous monkey, he shared his fruit with
all the other animals in the jungle. Each day the mango tree would
be surrounded by his friends: Lion, Hippopotamus, Zebra,
Giraffe, Tortoise and the others. They would chatter and joke
away, enjoying the fruit at the same time.

One day a crocodile swam up river and seeing the crowd of animals around the mango tree, he stopped a little way off to observe what was going on. Suddenly, Monkey saw Crocodile, whom he had never met before. Monkey invited him to taste his lovely mangoes.

'Would you like a mango?'

'I've never had one before,' replied Crocodile.

'Catch!' called Monkey.

Crocodile munched the mango and said,

'That was most delicious, thank you, Monkey.'

And so Monkey threw down many, many more mangoes. Crocodile stayed on for a long chat. From that day on Crocodile swam up river to visit Monkey every day and they became the best of friends.

One day as they were chatting about this and that, Crocodile mentioned that he lived with the crocodile tribe and that their great chief was very important and very clever. Monkey said,

'You should have told me about your chief before, so that I could send him a present of lovely juicy mangoes.'

Crocodile agreed that his chief would like to try the mangoes. So Monkey plucked plenty of mangoes and threw them into

Crocodile's open mouth. Crocodile swam back to his tribe with a mouthful of mangoes. He shared the mangoes with the chief and the other crocodiles in his tribe. He told them about his great new friend, Monkey.

The chief liked the mangoes very much. He asked Crocodile to bring more and Crocodile promised to bring some mangoes home every time he visited Monkey.

After a while, a thought occurred to the chief. 'If Monkey eats such delicious mangoes every day, what a delicious dinner Monkey would make.' If only he could get Monkey here. But, knowing how fond of Monkey Crocodile was, it would be difficult to have Monkey for his dinner. So the chief thought of a brilliant plan.

As Crocodile returned from his outing, the chief lay himself down at the bottom of the river and pretended to be very ill. Crocodile swam up to the chief and asked,

'What's the matter with you, my dear Chief?'

The chief replied, 'I am very ill and the Witch Doctor has told me that only the heart of a monkey can cure me. You must bring me a monkey's heart at once, otherwise I shall surely die.'

Crocodile was at a loss: where could he find a monkey's heart? Monkeys were difficult to catch. Then suddenly he remembered his friend, Monkey, living in the mango tree. Very sadly he thought to himself, 'Oh dear, oh dear, what shall I do? I love that little monkey, he is my great friend, but I also love my chief, he is my great leader and he will die if he doesn't eat the heart of a monkey.'

Poor Crocodile went round and round in circles trying to decide what to do, but in the end he thought that the chief was more important and that he would bring him Monkey's heart.

Early next morning, Crocodile set off to Monkey's home in the mango tree. All the way he was devising a plan. As usual, Monkey was delighted to see his friend.

'Hello there, my friend. I'm happy to see you this morning.'

Crocodile had made a good plan to catch Monkey and said,

'Monkey, you have been very kind to me these past few weeks, giving me and my tribe such wonderful fruit. I should like to do something for you in return.' Crocodile continued, 'For a long time I have wanted to invite you to my home across the river to meet my tribe and offer you hospitality. My chief would be very honoured to make your acquaintance.'

Monkey replied,

'How sweet of you to invite me to your home. I too would like to meet your chief and your tribe, but how can I get there? You live in the water, I would drown if I tried to go to your place. You see, dear Crocodile, I can't swim.'

'That's easily settled,' replied Crocodile. 'We live on the river bank as well as in the river. I can take you there; sit on my back and I'll ferry you across.'

Monkey agreed. He was happy that he had such a good friend as Crocodile. Monkey jumped down from the mango tree and landed on Crocodile's back. Crocodile swam across the river with Monkey sitting on his back. On reaching the middle of the river, Crocodile began to sink lower and lower into the water. He thought that it would be a good idea to drown Monkey before they got to his river bank. Down, down they went, deeper into the water. Monkey called out, 'I'm getting wet, Crocodile, please don't go down.'

There was silence as Crocodile continued to go down, down, deeper into the water. At once Monkey realised that something was wrong; he was very frightened. He cried out, 'What are you doing? I shall drown if you go down any further.' Crocodile replied, 'I cannot hide the truth from you, my dear friend. My chief is very ill and will die if he doesn't eat a monkey's heart.'

Monkey was shocked and terrified, he bit his lip to stop himself from crying while he thought of a plan to save himself. At last he said as calmly as he could,

'My friend, why didn't you tell me before that you needed my heart to save your chief? I would have brought it with me.'

'What! You don't have your heart with you?' asked Crocodile in surprise. 'No!' said Monkey. 'I always leave my heart in the mango tree when I go on a journey. Let's go back at once and get my heart for your chief.'

Crocodile turned round and quickly swam back to the mango tree. When they got there, Monkey jumped off Crocodile's back and hurried up the tree calling,

'You stupid crocodile, didn't you know that monkeys keep their hearts in their breast,

like everyone else? You foolish old crocodile, did you really
expect me to come back with you to your tribe to be killed?'

Monkey laughed and laughed.

'Go back to your tribe, our friendship is ended.'

Crocodile swam back down the river feeling very ashamed. He
shed a big crocodile tear as he realised how foolish he had been and
that now he had lost his best friend.

Monkey laughed and laughed and threw rotten mangoes
after the silly old crocodile.

All the animals in the jungle heard Monkey laugh
so loud that they came to see what it
was all about. They
surrounded the

mango tree and
listened to Monkey telling
them how he had out-witted
Crocodile, warning them never
to make friends with a crocodile if they
wanted to reach a good old age like Tortoise.

# SEDNA AND KING GULL

## CANADA

In a very cold place, where the land is ice and snow, and rocks and mountains; where the sea is forever raging and the winds howling; where the winters are long and dark; in this cold, harsh place live the Inuit people.

The Inuits tell many stories from a time when unbelievable things could happen. In those days fabulous spirits and magical creatures inhabited the frozen lands... Maybe they still do – who knows?

Sedna lived in this cold land. Sedna, known as Mother of the Sea, was once a mortal girl. She was a very beautiful girl with long, dark hair and large, dark eyes as black as the midnight sky. She lived in an igloo between the wild clouds and the freezing

   64

icebergs. She lived with her father – a brave, old hunter who devoted his life to bringing up his beloved daughter.

Sedna and her father both spent the long, dark winter hunting, cooking, drying animal skins and sewing clothes out of fur. In the spring, the sun made the icebergs sparkle and brought a little warmth and hope to the tribe. As some of the snow melted, flowers appeared, covering the ground with a rich carpet of blue and yellow, purple and white.

During these sparkling days, Sedna would run and play outside, not with other children but with the wild, free birds. She would dance to their flight and sing to their calling. Her very best friend was the king of the seagulls. He was very strong and beautiful, proud and powerful. He had huge wings and was covered with silver-grey feathers. His eyes shone like the stars in the sky. King Gull was greatly respected and deeply loved by the other birds in the kingdom.

There came a time when Sedna's father expected her to get married. Many young hunters came to court her. But Sedna was not interested in any of them.

Her father became worried. He would say, 'Sedna, I will not always be alive to hunt for you. It is time you chose a nice, young hunter who can take care of you. You must stop dreaming and dancing with the birds, they are not your kind.'

But Sedna would toss her raven-black hair and answer back, 'Dear father, there is not a man in the world that I want to marry.'

You see, in her heart, Sedna loved the king gull and wanted to marry him.

But she was afraid of upsetting her father and this made her sad. At the very moment Sedna was thinking these thoughts, the king gull flew overhead and saw her sadness. He felt a great warmth in his heart and also knew that he wanted to marry Sedna.

Using his magical powers, he turned himself into a man. Thus disguised, he came to the igloo and asked for Sedna's hand in marriage. Sedna was delighted; she could hardly contain her happiness when she recognised who this young man really was. Her father agreed to the match. And so it was that Sedna and the

   66

king gull were to leave her homeland and go to live in the place of the birds. Sedna kissed her father goodbye. He wished her good luck as he let her go for ever.

She came to the seafront where a kayak was waiting for her. She sat in the kayak and away they paddled to the far-off land of the birds. When at last they reached King Gull's kingdom, he led Sedna to his ice cave, which he had prepared for her, lining it with soft, white feathers. He also made her a thick blanket of feathers as fine as silk so that she would always keep warm. Sedna

67

was happy, learning new skills and discovering so many new friends.

One day, as she was gazing out to sea, she noticed a kayak in the distance. As it came closer she saw two young hunters, killing many birds aimlessly. Suddenly, out of the dark sky, King Gull flew in fury towards the kayak. He tried to stop the foolish boys. Flying above the kayak, then swooping low, his wings stiff and outstretched, he flew round and round shrieking wildly, trying to stop more slaughter.

But something terrible happened. One of the hunters aimed his spear at King Gull. It hit his grey body and pierced his heart. King Gull managed to fly towards Sedna and plunged at her feet.

With his last breath he said, 'Sedna, I have always loved you and always will. Please do this last thing for me. Take me out to sea and throw my body deep into the ocean. Only then will my magic work again, only then will we be together again in another life in another place.' With these words the beautiful seagull died.

Sedna was devastated, but through her tears she managed to find a kayak and gently placed her beloved bird inside. She paddled far out to sea. When they were far away she stopped and picked up her dear friend. She kissed King Gull and threw him

into the icy water. At that very moment the sky darkened, there was a flash of lightning and a clap of thunder. When Sedna looked up again the sky was full of birds; thousands and thousands of birds of every size and kind flew round and round, up and down, screeching and singing, 'King Gull is dead! King Gull is dead!'

Others were calling, 'Sea creatures are born! Sea creatures are born!' Sedna was very moved by this sight. Still crying, she leaned over the side of the kayak and looked deep into the sea. There she saw, to her amazement, the king gull transforming magically into a huge whale.

In this time of magic, as her tears were falling into the water they were transformed into walruses, seals, dolphins, octopuses, sea horses and fish and creatures of every kind.

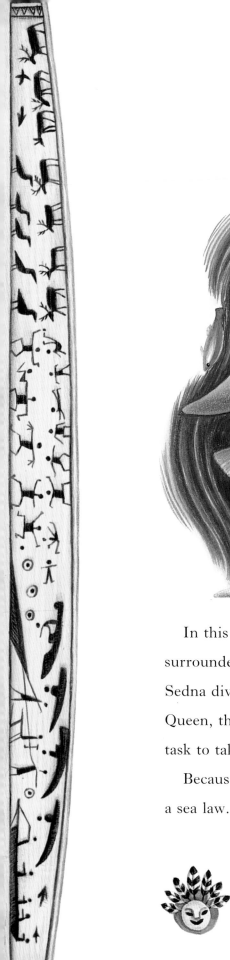

In this moment of magic the sea creatures came to be. They all surrounded the kayak as if to say, 'Join us, Sedna, be our Queen.' Sedna dived into the icy water and she did indeed become the Sea Queen, the Sea Spirit, Mother of the Oceans. It was now Sedna's task to take care of all the sea creatures of the world.

Because of the hunters' cruelty in killing aimlessly, Sedna made a sea law. Hunters were only permitted to hunt for food and skins

and only as much as they needed for their tribe to survive and no more. If this law was ever broken, Sedna would call up fierce storms, the sea would swell and rage, thus preventing men from hunting. Then only if the shaman of the tribe dived into the sea and swam down to visit Sedna under the water, giving her news of the Inuit people, only then would she calm the sea again so that hunting could resume.

# MAGIC IN THE RAINFOREST

BRAZIL

There was a time in the old days when there was no darkness, no night, no sleep. In that time there was only light, only day, only waking. But the great old trees that lived in the rainforest knew many things. It was their wisdom that first brought night out of the river, into the world.

The old trees cast their magic far and wide across the rainforest. As they did so, all living creatures were born. The sticks and the roots in the forest turned into animals. The leaves on the trees turned into birds. The stones and pebbles in the rivers turned into fish and snails. The toucan, the quetzal, the humming bird and the parrot were made. The armadillo, the anteater, the tapir and the jaguar were made. The snake, the piranha and the turtle were made. It all happened in that very moment when the old trees brought night to the earth.

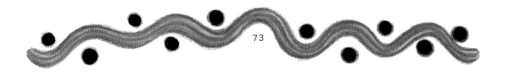

In the darkness, Snake slithered along the river bank
looking at his beautiful eyes reflected in the water. As he did so,
he sang:

> 'Eyes, eyes, sparkling bright
>
> Dance for me
>
> In the magic of the night.'

And his eyes popped out of his head and danced on the surface
of the water.

At that very moment, Jaguar was walking along the river bank
looking at his beautiful body reflected in the water. All of a
sudden he noticed Snake's eyes dancing on the surface of
the water.

He lay down in the long grass perfectly still, perfectly silent,
and watched. After a while, Snake sang,

> 'Eyes, eyes, twinkling bright
>
> Dance back to me
>
> In the magic of the night.'

And his eyes danced back across the surface of the water
straight into his head.

Jaguar was amazed by what he had just seen. He went up to
Snake and asked, 'How can you do this wonderful thing?'

Snake, rather pleased at a chance of showing off, repeated his
song. Again, his eyes popped out of his head and, like fireflies,
they danced all over the river in the moonlight. After a while

Snake sang once more and his eyes danced back to him.

Jaguar was even more amazed. He said, 'I would like my eyes to dance like that. Please teach me the trick.' Snake agreed but warned, 'This is no trick, this is magic and magic can be dangerous!' But Jaguar didn't care, he just wanted his eyes to dance on the water. So Snake began to sing,

'Jaguar's eyes, sparkling bright

Dance for him

In the magic of the night.'

And sure enough, Jaguar's eyes popped out of his head and danced across the river. After a while, Snake sang,

> 'Jaguar's eyes, twinkling bright
>
> Dance back to him
>
> In the magic of the night.'

Jaguar was so thrilled, he wanted another turn. 'That was wonderful – do it again.'

'No, it's not safe,' replied Snake.

'Please, please, do it again, just once more,' pleaded Jaguar.

Snake gave in. But this time, as Jaguar's eyes were dancing on the water, he sang,

> 'Jaguar's eyes, twinkling bright
>
> Dance back to ME
>
> In the magic of the night.'

And, as Jaguar's eyes came dancing towards Snake, his tongue flicked out and swallowed the eyes. He turned and slithered away

into the forest, into the night. Poor Jaguar couldn't see anything;
frightened and lonely, he wandered through the forest, not knowing
where he was going, not knowing what he was to do. Unable to hunt
without his eyes, he was doomed to starve to death. In his despair,
he lay down under a wise old tree. He put his paws over his empty
eye sockets and moaned softly.

The tree felt very sorry for Jaguar. He decided
to help the sad animal.
Using his magical
powers he called
for his friend
Harpy Eagle.

Harpy Eagle
came flying by and hovered just above Jaguar. 'Why are you so sad?'
she asked. Jaguar told her the strange story. The bird said, 'Yes, these
are indeed strange times. In the darkness of the night, many mysterious
things can happen. Wait here, and I will see what I can do to help.'
With these words, Harpy Eagle flew over the forest and far away,
looking, listening until her keen eyes spied Snake slithering towards
a lake. Harpy Eagle flew up to Snake. Hovering above him, she said,

'I have heard that you can make your eyes dance over the water.'

'Yes,' replied Snake. 'That's true.'

Harpy Eagle said, 'I find it very hard to believe. It is surely
not possible.'

'With magic, everthing is possible,' replied Snake.

'I don't really believe in magic. If it is true, why don't you show me how your eyes dance over the water?' asked Harpy Eagle.

Snake, rather pleased at a chance of showing off, sang his song,

> 'Eyes, eyes sparkling bright
>
> Dance for me
>
> In the magic of the night.'

And sure enough his eyes popped out of his head and danced over the lake. Harpy Eagle, hovering above the water, instantly swooped down and caught both eyes in her beak and flew off back into the forest, back into the night and arrived at the wise old tree where Jaguar was still waiting.

Harpy Eagle hovered above Jaguar's head, she aimed and

dropped both eyes perfectly into the sockets in Jaguar's head.

Jaguar could see again; in fact, he could see better and further than before. He looked at his reflection in the river, and was astonished how beautiful and bright his new eyes were.

'Thank you, my friend. How can I repay you?' he said.

'I am very hungry; why don't you hunt me a tapir, my favourite meat?' replied Harpy Eagle.

So Jaguar caught a large tapir and the two new friends enjoyed a delicious feast.

Ever since that night Jaguar has always left a part of his kill for Harpy Eagle in gratitude for his sparkling new eyes. And as for Snake's eyes, they grew back again, staring, glaring, shining bright, but never again to dance in the magic of the night.

# SOURCES FOR THE STORIES

I am a storyteller. I travel from community to community, from school to school, from theatre to theatre and from country to country telling the stories which I have collected throughout my life.

I started telling stories when I was a little girl, first to my brother, our dog and cat, then to my friends and neighbours, and I've been telling stories ever since. Most of my stories come from the oral tradition of storytelling. I hear them from other storytellers, from friends or from people I meet in life. Some of my stories come from collections in books. These are the ways in which I found the stories in *The Barefoot Book of Animal Tales*.

### GRANDMOTHER SPIDER (USA)

I read this Cherokee story in *Storymaking in Education and Therapy*, published by Jessica Kingsley. I adapted it and I often tell it to schoolchildren during book weeks.

### THE RABBIT IN THE MOON (INDIA)

I was invited to tell stories from around the world at a United Nations conference on world faiths held in London in November 1992. After the session, a Buddhist monk called Dayatmananda invited me to the Ramakrishna Vedanta Centre in Buckinghamshire to share stories with him. During this meeting he told me the story 'The Rabbit in the Moon' and I loved it. Now it is a story I often tell.

### THE DRAGON AND THE COCKEREL (CHINA)

I heard this story at the Chinese Community Centre, Soho, London, in 1984 when I ran a workshop on shadow puppets for the Chinese New Year. Weng Naigiang, one of the participants, created the most delightful shadow play using the tale of 'The Dragon and the Cockerel'.

### THE GREEDY FROG (AUSTRALIA)

In 1993 there was an exhibition of Aboriginal paintings at the Hayward Gallery, London. There I met Wendy Watson, an Aborigine storyteller. We sat under one of the paintings and she told me a few stories from her people. 'The Greedy Frog' was one of these.

### THE MUSICIANS OF BREMEN (GERMANY)

This was one of my favourite stories when I was a small child. My grandfather told it to me at bedtime. I later found it in *Grimm's Fairy Tales*.

### NEVER TRUST A PELICAN (THAILAND)

This story was performed as a mime show by an Asian mime and dance company at Tara Arts Centre in south-west London in 1982. I then adapted the story to be told with words and movement.

### THE MONKEY'S HEART (KENYA)

I heard this story at an 'African village' festival held in Kew Gardens, London, in 1988. At this occasion many artists from all over Africa were invited to create villages and provide entertainment typical of their particular country. Kofi Oswaggo, a marvellous storyteller from Kenya, told many stories, including 'The Monkey's Heart'. He explained that the stories are tribal and each tribe has their own version of similar tales. The story in this collection is from Kenya but is also found in other versions in Tanzania and Ghana.

### SEDNA AND KING GULL (CANADA)

I met two Inuit throat singers at a storytelling festival at the Queen Elizabeth Hall, London, in 1984. I can't remember their names, but they were both very tiny women who made the most extraordinary sounds with their throats. They sounded rather like whales and dolphins, seals and seagulls. At a party after the show, we exchanged stories and they told me the tale of 'Sedna and King Gull'.

### MAGIC IN THE RAINFOREST (BRAZIL)

I met a Brazilian Indian, Inti Ramos, in 1986 at the Museum of Mankind, London, where I was telling stories about the North American Indians. She had come to London to learn English and to go to film school. We spent a few wonderful days walking in the Welsh hills and exchanging stories from our different cultures. One of the stories Inti told me was 'Magic in the Rainforest'.